For Briony and Simon
A.M.

_____

For John and Alexander
P.L.

First published 1987 by Walker Books Ltd., London

Text copyright © 1988, 1987 by Adrian Mitchell
Illustrations copyright © 1987 by Priscilla Lamont

Requests for permission to make copies of any part of the work
should be mailed to: Permissions,
Harcourt Brace Jovanovich, Publishers, Orlando, Florida 32887.

Library of Congress Cataloging-in-Publication Data
Mitchell, Adrian, 1932 –
Our mammoth goes to school.
Summary: The Gumble twins take their pet mammoth to school,
causing quite a spectacle both there and on the class trip
to the Animal Park.   [1. Mammoth–Fiction.   2. Schools–Fiction.
3. School excursions–Fiction.   4. Zoos–Fiction.
5. Twins–Fiction]   1. Lamont, Priscilla, ill.   II. Title.
PZ7.M6850q   1987   E   87-11951
ISBN 0-15-258837-X

Printed and bound by L.E.G.O., Vicenza, Italy
First U.S. edition 1988   A B C D E

Our Mammoth
Goes to School

Written by
Adrian Mitchell

Illustrated by
Priscilla Lamont

HARCOURT BRACE JOVANOVICH, PUBLISHERS

SAN DIEGO   NEW YORK   LONDON

We are the Gumble Twins,
Bing and Saturday Gumble.
We have a book called

How to Look After Your Mammoth.

It says, "Mammoths are clever.
Mammoths like to learn."
So our Mom, Sally Gumble, said,
"Better take Buttercup to school."

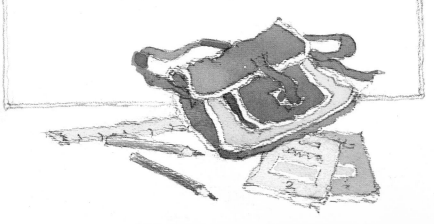

We rode Buttercup into
   the playground.
All the children cheered.
Out came both our teachers.
We have a good funny teacher
   called Lucy Moose.
Lucy Moose fetched Buttercup
   a bucket of milk.

We have a bad sad teacher
  called Mr. Binko.
Mr. Binko frowned and said,
"No mammoths allowed in my school."
Lucy Moose smiled and said,
"We'll have our history lesson
  out in the playground."

She told us a story of the old days
    when there were
    hundreds of mammoths.
At playtime we all used Buttercup
    as a jungle gym.
We used her curving tusks for slides.
Buttercup purred like a motorboat.

Mr. Binko stared and said,
"That mammoth has fleas.
    They are big as sparrows
    but not as pretty."
Saturday said, "They are only
    mammoth fleas.
    They won't itch people."

Bing said, "She only has four fleas.
We call them Whizzby, Fizzby,
Thisbe and Chips."
We said, "All mammoths have fleas.
They are fond of their fleas.
A mammoth with no fleas is lonely."

Mr. Binko grinned and said,
"Everybody ready for the School Trip?
    Today we're going to the Animal Park.
    But we're not taking Buttercup
    or Bing or Saturday Gumble
    because of those dirty fleas."

Lucy Moose said, "Sorry,
  you'd better go home."
We climbed up on to Buttercup's back.
But when the school bus drove away
  Buttercup started to follow it.
Have you ever been for
  a wild mammoth ride?

We shouted out, "Stop!"
But nothing would stop her.
We hung on tight to the hair on
        the hump behind her head.
                She went bumping along,
                    faster and faster,
                    past bikes, past cars.

First she went
        Gerlumpergumper.

Then she went
        Lottentotten
        Lottentotten.

Then she went
        Snoppitter
            Poppitter
        Snoppitter
            Poppitter.

Then she went Ballooby Ballooby
  Ballooby Ballooby Ballooby Ballooby
  all the way to the Animal Park.

Buttercup thundered into the park.
Past merry monkeys,

past curious camels,

past a terrible tiger,

past zigzag zebras.

Buttercup slowed down beside a field.
There were eight elephants eating hay.
Buttercup lifted up her trunk
    and made a sound like
    a big brass band.
All the elephants came to meet her
    blowing on their trumpets.
The elephants crowded
    round Buttercup.
They sniffed her.
They patted her.
They gazed into her
    brown and golden eyes.
They all made a noise
    that sounded like "Yes".
Then they led Buttercup
    down to a lake.

Buttercup and the elephants
    sploshed into the water.
They played Fountains.
They played Underwater
    Hide-and-Seek.
They played Musical Mudbaths.
We played too and got
    wet as walruses.
But we didn't mind.

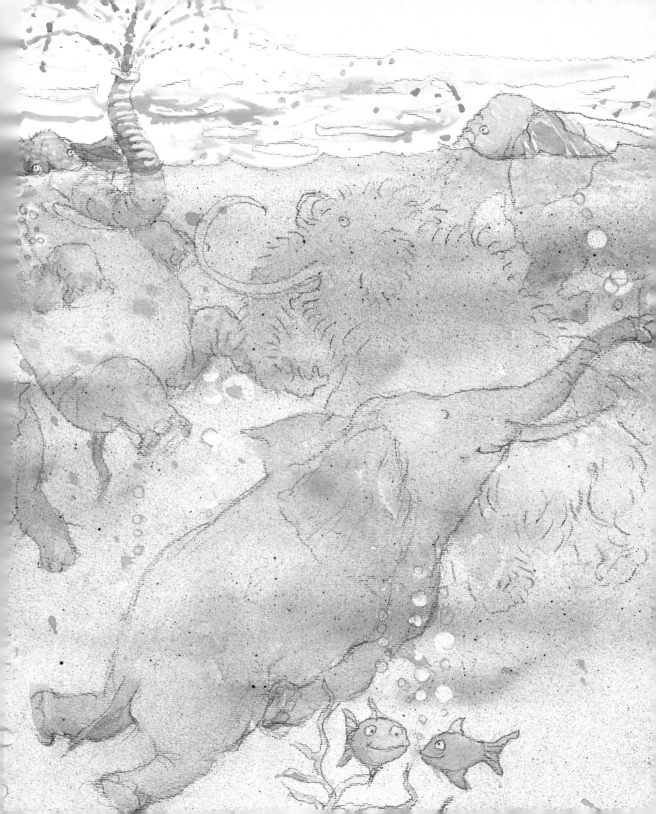

Then the School Trip found us.
Lucy Moose gave Buttercup
    a bunch of dandelions.
But Mr. Binko laughed at Buttercup.
"Great hairy monster with fleas," he said.
He laughed so much his wig
    fell in a puddle.

We picked up his wig and
    handed it back.
We nearly burst,
    but we didn't laugh.
But Buttercup shook and
    snuffled a bit
    and so did Lucy Moose.

When we got home we told our Mom.
She promised to take Buttercup
    every Sunday to visit
    her friends at the Animal Park.
We had beans for supper.
Buttercup had six buckets of soup.
Her fleas had tomato juice.
Then we went to bed
    and we slept like beanbags.